FOREST PARK PUBLIC LIBRARY

3 2026 00350 7982

W9-AMA-955

DATE DUE

		OCT 2014	

E
Hoena   Hoena, B. A.
         The black hole report

FOREST PARK PUBLIC LIBRARY

EEK & ACK

THE BLACK HOLE REPORT

written by
BLAKE A. HOENA

illustrations by
STEVE HARPSTER

FOREST PARK PUBLIC LIBRARY

OCT — 2014

FOREST PARK, IL.

STONE ARCH BOOKS
a capstone imprint

Eek and Ack Early Chapter Books
is published by Stone Arch Books,
A Capstone Imprint
1710 Roe Crest Drive
North Mankato, Minnesota 56003
www.capstonepub.com

Copyright © 2014 Stone Arch Books

All rights reserved. No part of this publication may be reproduced
in whole or in part, or stored in a retrieval system, or transmitted
in any form or by any means, electronic, mechanical, photocopying,
recording, or otherwise, without written permission of the publisher.

Library of Congress Cataloging-in-Publication Data
Hoena, B. A., author.
 The black hole report / by Blake A. Hoena; illustrated by Steve
Harpster.
     pages cm. — (Eek and Ack: early chapter books)
 Summary: While researching black holes for Ack's homework report,
the brothers get sucked into one and end up in a scary universe.
ISBN 978-1-4342-6409-1 (hardcover)
ISBN 978-1-4342-6554-8 (paperback)
ISBN 978-1-4342-9235-3 (ebook)
 1. Extraterrestrial beings—Juvenile fiction. 2. Brothers—Juvenile
fiction. 3. Black holes (Astronomy)—Juvenile fiction. 4. Homework—
Juvenile fiction. [1. Extraterrestrial beings—Fiction. 2. Brothers—
Fiction. 3. Black holes (Astronomy)—Fiction. 4. Homework—Fiction. 5.
Science fiction.] I. Harpster, Steve, illustrator. II. Title.
 PZ7.H67127Bl 2014
 813.6—dc23
                                          2013028214

Printed in China by Nordica.
1013/CA21301915
092013   007743NORDS14

TABLE OF CONTENTS

Chapter 1
HOMEWORK..........................5

Chapter 2
EEK HELPS ACK....................11

Chapter 3
THE Z UNIVERSE...................15

Chapter 1

HOMEWORK

Ack liked school. Galaxy exploration class was his favorite subject.

Today in class, he would get to learn about a strange, new place.

"Students, I am going to hand out your research homework," Mrs. Grym said.

Ack could barely sit still. He was so excited.

"I will give each of you a space object to explore," Mrs. Grym said.

"That will be fun," Ack thought. "Maybe I'll get to visit a planet where people speak in armpit noises. I can already toot the alphabet up to P!"

"After you are done, you will write a 100-page paper on what you learned," Mrs. Grym added. "Now everyone, come get your subjects."

The students rushed to the front of the class.

Mrs. Grym handed Ack a piece of paper with two words on it.

"Black hole!" Ack shouted. "But I don't know anything about black holes."

"That's why it's called research," Mrs. Grym said.

BBRRRIIINNGGG!

The final bell rang. Class was over. The other students jumped up and raced for the door.

Ack walked slowly to his bus.

Chapter 2

EEK HELPS ACK

Ack slumped down in the seat
behind his brother, Eek.

"What's wrong?" Eek asked.

"I have to write a report on black
holes," Ack said. "I don't know a
thing about black holes."

Eek grabbed Ack's sheet of paper.
He got a big grin on his face.

"This gives me an idea!" he said.

"Oh, no," Ack said. His stomach
started to hurt. "Your ideas always
scare me."

"Do you want help with your homework or not?" Eek asked.

"Um . . . I guess so," Ack said.

Ack wasn't sure if he trusted his brother. But he did need help.

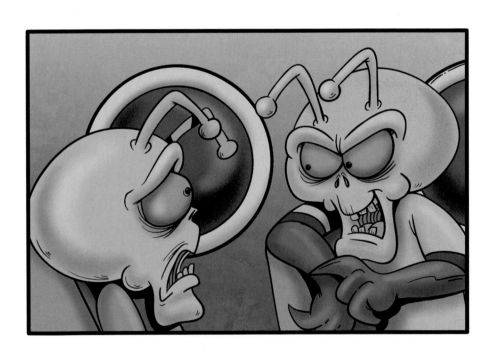

As they got off the bus, Eek told
Ack his plan. "You need to see a
black hole with your own eyes. And
I know just where to find one," he
said.

Chapter 3

THE Z UNIVERSE

Eek and Ack raced to their spaceship. They climbed in, blasted off, and headed to the black hole.

"So why are you really helping me?" Ack asked. "I don't believe you are just being nice."

"I wanted to test my new whizzler drive," Eek said. "Hold on!"

Their spaceship zipped across the galaxy. Soon, they reached the black hole. Rocks and space junk swirled around them.

"Let's get closer," Ack said.

"Ack, stop!" Eek shouted. "Don't you know anything about black holes?"

"No, that's why I'm doing research," Ack said.

"They're like giant vacuums," Eek said.

But it was too late. They flew too close. The black hole sucked up their spaceship and threw it around.

"Aaaahhhh!" Eek and Ack screamed.

When their spaceship shot out the other side of the black hole, another spaceship appeared.

Two pink and fuzzy creatures were inside the other spaceship. Their voices echoed through a speaker.

"Welcome to the Z universe," one of them said.

"We're Zeek and Zack," the other said.

Then together they yelled, "Do you need a hug?"

The pink creatures grinned out at Eek and Ack's spaceship.

Two big furry arms reached out
and hugged Eek and Ack's spaceship.

"Eek!" Ack screamed.

"Ack!" Eek cried.

"They are pink and fuzzy!" they
shouted together. "And they're
hugging us!"

"Fire the shove-a-tron," Eek told Ack.

Slam! The shove-a-tron pushed Zeek and Zack's spaceship away.

"Wait! Come back. Let's hug some more," Zeek and Zack said happily.

"Ah!" Eek and Ack cried in horror.

Eek spun their spaceship around.

He headed back into the black hole.

"Let's get out of here!" yelled Eek.

"But I didn't get to do any research," Ack said. "I'm going to get a Z on my report!"

"Hey, that's the same grade I got on mine," Eek said.

"Oh, no!" Ack said. "It's even worse than I thought!"

ABOUT THE AUTHOR

Blake A. Hoena once spent a whole weekend just watching his favorite science-fiction movies. Those movies made him wonder why those aliens, with their death rays and hyper-drives, couldn't actually conquer Earth. That's when he created Eek and Ack, who play at conquering Earth like earthling kids play at stopping bad guys. Blake has written more than twenty books for children, and currently lives in Minneapolis, Minnesota.

ABOUT THE ARTIST

Steve Harpster has loved to draw funny cartoons, mean monsters, and goofy gadgets since he was able to pick up a pencil. In first grade, he avoided writing assignments by working on the pictures for stories instead. Steve was able to land a job drawing funny pictures for books, and that's really what he's best at. Steve lives in Columbus, Ohio, with his wonderful wife, Karen, and their sheepdog, Doodle.

GLOSSARY

black hole (BLAK HOHL)—an area in space that sucks in everything around it

exploration (ek-splor-AY-shuhn)—the act of studying something or somewhere unknown

explore (ek-SPLOR)—to travel in order to discover what a place is like

galaxy (GAL-uhk-see)—a large group of stars and planets

horror (HOR-ur)—great fear or shock

research (REE-surch)—the act of collecting information about something

shove-a-tron (SHUV-uh-trahn)—a long armlike machine on Eek and Ack's spaceship that is used to push away dangerous things

slumped (SLUHMPD)—sank down heavily

swirled (SWURLD)—moved around in circles

vacuums (VAK-yooms)—machines that pick up dirt from carpets

whizzler drive (WHIZ-luhr DRIVE)—a machine on planet Gloop that makes alien spaceships go very fast

TALK ABOUT THE STORY

1. Ack did not like his research topic. Have you ever been given an assignment at school that you didn't like at first? Was it as bad as you expected?

2. What space object would you like to explore? Why?

3. Eek offers to help Ack in the story. Do you help your siblings? Do they help you?

WRITING TIME

1. Do your own research about black holes and write a paragraph about what you've learned.

2. Pretend you are in a galaxy exploration class, and you get to travel to outer space. Write a story about what you see.

3. Compare Eek and Ack to Zeek and Zack. Make a list of similarities and differences.

EXPLORING THE UNIVERSE
with Eek & Ack

It's no surprise that Ack was worried about his research topic. Black holes are difficult to study.

These places in space have very, very strong gravity. Gravity is a force that pulls things in. Anything that comes too close to a black hole will be pulled in and disappear, even light.

A black hole is formed from a dying star. As a star's gases burn, heat pushes out from the star into space. Then the star's gravity pulls the heat back in.

But when a star gets older, it runs out of gases. The heat stops pushing out from the star, but gravity keeps pulling in. The star gets smaller and smaller, until it seems to disappear. What's left is a black hole.

The scientists who study black holes have a hard job. Black holes are billions of miles away. They are also invisible. If scientists tried to send up special machines to get a closer look at the black holes, the gravity would damage the machines.

So scientists have to study the area surrounding the black hole. They use special telescopes to see what happens to things around the black hole.

THE FUN DOESN'T STOP HERE!

DISCOVER MORE AT...
www.CAPSTONEKIDS.com

FIND COOL WEBSITES AND MORE
BOOKS LIKE THIS ONE AT WWW.FACTHOUND.COM.
JUST TYPE IN THE BOOK ID: 9781434264091
AND YOU'RE READY TO GO!